7+

The Usborne Book of SILLY JOKES

written and compiled by
Philip Hawthorn
Designed by Russell Punter
Illustrated by Kim Blundell

WITHDRAWN

D0715004

What's got two humps and is found on the moon?

A lost camel.

WHAT'S THIS?

Turn over the page to find out!

Q. What do cats have for breakfast?

Why were the rabbits eating in the middle of the road?
It was a dual cabbage-way.

How do you make a Mexican chilli?
Send him to the North Pole.

Why did the tomato go red?
Because it saw the salad dressing.

What do you give a sick lemon?
Lemonade.

What cheese is made backwards?
Edam.

What's red and as tall as a tree?
A strawberry on stilts.

Why are cooks bullies?
Because they beat eggs, whip cream, and mash potatoes.

What's that?

A box of corn flakes going up stairs.

What's orange and sounds like a parrot?
A carrot.

NEWSFLASH

A man is in hospital after eating a bag of daffodil bulbs. Police say he'll be out next spring.

Smelly-vision

Why do my friends call me a vampire?
Just eat your soup before it clots.

Why have you got custard in one ear and jelly in the other?
Speak up, I'm a trifle deaf.

What do you call a chef with a banana in each ear?
Anything you like, he can't hear you.

What cake is very clean?
A bath bun.

What cake gives you an electric shock?
A current bun.

What's a boxer's favourite cake?
A ring doughnut.

Iced bun

Iced bunny

If a frozen bun is an iced bun, what's frozen ink?
Iced ink.
Pooh!

Puffed wheat

What's the fastest cake in world?
'Scone.

Two eggs climbing a pyramid.

Shall I tell you the joke about margarine?
Butter not, you might spread it.

What's green and ticks?
A clockwork cucumber.

What do you get if you cross a pig with zebra?
Stripy sausages.
Looks like my brother.

Did you hear about the stupid ghost?
He bumped into a door.

Why do witches ride on broomsticks?
Because vacuum cleaners haven't got long enough cords.

Why do pyramids have horns instead of doorbells?
So you can toot-and-come-in.

Is mummy in?

How do you get into a locked coffin?
Using a skeleton key.

There once was a woman from Ryde,
Who ate ninety apples and died.
The apples fermented
Inside the lamented,
And made cider inside 'er inside.

Where do American Indian ghosts live?
In a creepy teepee.

Boo!

What do you call a ghostly feline?
Scaredy-cat.

What do you get if you cross a Boy Scout with a monster?
Something that scares old ladies across the road.

DOCTOR DOCTOR

I think I'm dead.
It must be the coffin.

Heard the joke about the snow-ghost?
You'll be scared stiff.

Haunted Housemusic

What dance do ghosts do best?
Boo-gie.

What has webbed feet and fangs?
Count Quackula.

I like a nice skele-tan.

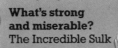

Lazy bones

What was the skeleton gangster called?
Al Ca-bone.

What do you get if you cross a monster with a canary?
A big yellow thing that goes "TWEET!!"

TWEET!

This is my family photograph.

NEWSFLASH

All the ghosts in England are on strike. Here's a report from our spooksman.

What's strong and miserable?
The Incredible Sulk

What's the first thing a monster eats after it's had a tooth out?
The dentist.

I can't tell witch is witch.

A banana sneezing.

THE HAUNTED HOUSE by HUGO FIRST

INVESTIGATING GHOSTS by DENISE R. KNOCKING

DEADLY JOKES by Di Laffin

Terrible Nightmare BY GLADYS OVER

Book Worm

When will I die? BY Sue Nora Later

FAMOUS FRIGHTS by TERRY FIED

That's Wick-ed!

Q. What cake makes a baker shake?

What music do florists like?
Heavy petal.

Why did the duck become a ballerina?
To dance in the "Nut-quacker".

What is a pirate's favourite toy?
A yo-ho-ho-yo.

What do you call a comedian who only tells jokes for 60 seconds?
Jester Minute.

KEN U. SEETHIS OPTICIAN

Have your eyes ever been checked?

No, always blue.

Spy scraper

U. NAMITT GENERAL STORES

Get me an axe, and make it choppy.

I chopped the wrong tree down this morning.

Must have been an axe-ident.

Long arm of the law

SWAG

A criminal record

Knock, knock!
Who's there?
Police.
Police who?
Police open the door, I'm freezing.

NEWSFLASH

A thief today stole the world's largest pair of braces: it was the biggest hold up for years. Police are searching for a man with a red bike: if they don't find him soon they'll use a car.

What do you call a flying policeman?
A helicopper.

What's the difference between a church bell and a thief?
One peals from the steeple, the other steals from the people.

What did the crook who stole the calender get?
Twelve months.

What thief steals meat?
A hamburglar.

Why did the bank robber saw the legs off his bed?
Because he wanted to lie low.

What do you call a detective in a bubble bath?
Sherlock Foams.

Spy-der

A dead one of these.

MAKING HONEY by B. Keeper

The PLUMBER'S HANDBOOK by Lee King

GERMAN BARBERS by Herr Dresser

SUCCESSFUL PLAYS by Stan D. Novation

BEING A POLICE OFFICER by Laura Norder

THE DOUBTFUL AUTHOR by Ken I. Wright

CLOAKROOM ATTENDANTS by Angus McCoatup

HOW TO BE ARRESTED by Kermit Crimes

Q. How do you start a flower race?

What's the smelliest game?
Ping pong.

Why are babies good at soccer?
Because they are expert dribblers.

What's got feathers, ticks and is hit regularly?
A shuttle-clock.

What do you call a broken go-kart?
A stop-kart.

What's an electric eel's favourite game?
Ice shock-ey.

What's blue and furry, and does 80mph?
A cold gerbil on skis.

What's the difference between a bad wrestler and a bad electrician?
One loses fights, the other fuses lights.

When are racing cars like cats?
When they are lapping.

What a purr-fect joke.

Why were the arrows nervous?
Because they were in a quiver.

What do you get if you cross a chess piece with Chinese food?
A pawn cracker.

If you have an umpire in tennis and a referee in football, what do you get in bowls?
Goldfish.

Why are baseball fields so valuable?
Because they have a diamond in the middle.

What ring is square?
A boxing ring.

DOCTOR DOCTOR

I'm a wrestler and I feel awful.
Get a grip on yourself.

I think I'm a tennis racket.
You're too highly strung.

I keep thinking I'm a pack of cards.
Sit down and I'll deal with you later.

I keep thinking I'm a billiard ball.
Get to end of the cue.

My nose keeps running.
Well lock it up then.

NEWSFLASH

Rex, the champion dog, is missing. Police say they have no lead on him.

KNOCK! KNOCK! WHO'S THERE?

Judo.
Judo who?
Judo I gotta cold.

JO JITSU Martial Arts Instructor

Did you hear about the man who went fly fishing?
He caught a 3lb bluebottle.

What's a jockey's favourite country?
Horse-tralia

Why don't giants like polo?
Because they prefer po-high.

Why does a golfer carry two pairs of trousers?
In case he gets a hole in one.

Why did two elephants not enter the swimming race?
They'd only one pair of trunks.

Why was the athlete in trouble?
Because she was for the high jump.

A worms eye view of an early bird.

WORLD'S WORST SHOT by Mrs De-Target

THE RACE by Willie Wynn and Betty Does

I've got an enormous pack of cards.
Big deal.

Mice Skating

I keep racing pigeons
Do you ever win?

Where do computers sit at school?

How was the naughty train punished?
It had to write railway lines.

Why did the toad visit the mushroom?
Because it was a toad-school.

What do you call a vampire adding numbers?
Counter Dracula.

How do you know if a hippo is sitting next to you at school?
He has an 'H' on his pencil case.

What's a butterfly's favourite lesson?
Moth-ematics.

What disease do art teachers get?
Pencilitis.

REGISTER	
NAME	
Eileen	A girl with one long leg and one short leg
Oscar	A boy who is a world famous actor
Wanda	A girl who sleep walks
Claude	A boy who keeps a wild tiger
Berna-dette	A girl who throws gas bills on the fire
Beatrix	A girl who balances 3 pints of beer on her head
Cliff	A boy with a face like a rock
Ingrid	A girl with her foot in a drain
Bob	A boy who can't swim

Which English king was good at fractions?
Henry 1/8th.

What do donkeys enjoy best at school?
Ass-embly.

What sum is done underwater?
An octoplus.

What's the definition of impeccable?
Something that can't be eaten by chickens.

What's the definition of a volcano?
A mountain with hiccups.

How do mushrooms count?
On their fungus.

A spider doing a pole vault.

What's the most popular food in heaven?
Angel cakes.

What's hairy and sneezes?
A coconut with a cold.

What's a bee's favourite sweet?
Bumble gum.

Where do sheep eat in the summer?
At a baa-beque.

Why was the peppermint in the Olympics?
Because it was a mint-ernational.

How do shellfish take pictures?
With a clam-era.

KNOCK! KNOCK! WHO'S THERE?

Olive.
Olive who?
Olive here, let me in.

Soup.
Soup who?
Superman.

A potato.
A potato who?
A potato clock I was this morning.

Toffee.
Toffee who?
Toffee tums in a tup.

A sick note

A Fez-ant

WAITER! WAITER!

How long will my sausages be?
About five inches sir.

Why have you got food all over your jacket?
You said to lay on a feast, so I did.

Is there tomato soup on the menu?
There was, but I wiped it off.

This pie doesn't taste right.
That's why it's left.

What's red and white and goes up and down?
A tomato sandwich on a pogo stick.

What looks like half a lemon?
The other half.

What's yellow, has big teeth and lives in the refrigerator?
Butter, I lied about the teeth.

What's the definition of a redcurrant?
An embarrassed blackcurrant.

Why are bananas good gymnasts?
Because they're often in splits.

I always drink cocoa in my pyjamas.

Don't they get a bit soggy?

CHIPS FROM EXOTIC COUNTRIES by Sultan Vinegar

THE EVERLASTING ICE CREAM by Trudy Light

EGG RECIPES by Sue Flay

DOCTOR DOCTOR

I think I'm a dumpling.
You are in a stew.

I feel like a burger.
Me too. Here's some money, go and get them.

I keep thinking I'm a spoon.
Just sit there and don't stir.

I feel like an apple.
Cor!

I keep thinking I can smell pepper.
That must get up your nose.

One day I think I'm an onion, the next a tomato.
You're in a bit of a pickle, then.

What's the favourite food of . . .

A hedgehog?
A spine-apple.

I thought it was a prickled onion.

A deer?
Doe-nuts.

A drummer?
Beat-root.

A hairdresser?
Par-snips.

A bricklayer?
Wall-nuts.

A hot cat?
Mice cream.

A tea-spoon?
Lob-stir.

A washing machine?
Spin-ach.

(14)

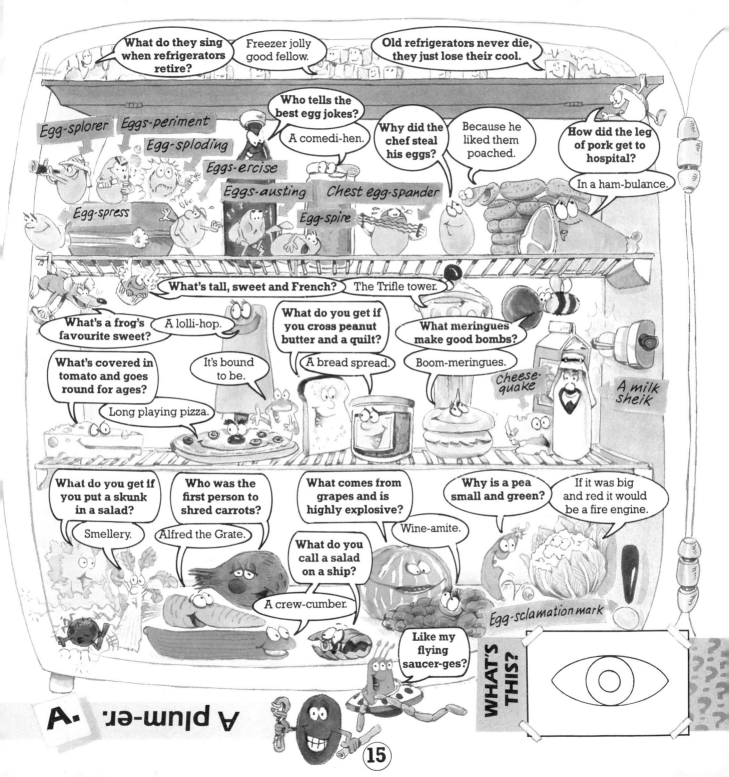

What's red, hot and travels at 150 mph?
A turbo radish.

How do lobsters get to work?
In a taxi crab.

What's black and white and has eight wheels?
A penguin on roller skates.

Where are Chinese car horns made?
Hong King.

Why did the baby put wheels on its cradle?
Because it wanted to rock and roll.

What happens to broken down frogs?
They get toad away.

How do fleas travel?
They itch-hike.

What does Corporal Goldfish drive?
A tank.

What's the difference between a big hill and a big pill?
One's hard to get up, the other's hard to get down.

What did the traffic lights say to the traffic?
Don't look, I'm changing.

How did the bride get to her wedding?
On her train.

What do you call a stupid boat?
An idi-yacht.

NEWSFLASH

A ship carrying a cargo of yo-yos has hit an iceberg. It sank 46 times.

A truck carrying glue has overturned. Police say they are completely stuck.

A van loaded with strawberries has collided with another carrying sugar. There is now a huge jam.

Today some thieves hijacked a truck carrying wigs. Police are combing the area.

What did the sardine say when it saw a submarine?
Look, canned people.

What would you get if Batman and Robin were run over by a steamroller?
Flatman and Ribbon.

How do you know that planes are scared of the dark?
Because they have to leave the landing lights on.

LONG WALK HOME by Mr Lars Buss

OUR CAR'S BROKEN by Sarah McCannick

BREAKDOWN TRUCKS — by — Tony Carslately

CRASH LANDING by Claire de Run way

MY LIFE IN SUBMARINES by Perry Scope

STOLEN VEHICLES by Nick McCarr

DOCTOR DOCTOR

I've been terribly run down.
Did you get the car's number?

I feel like the back of a car.
You're exhausted.

What do you get if you cross . . .

A supersonic jet with a roll of sticky tape?
Something that breaks the sound barrier then mends it again.

A police car's light with a fried egg?
A flash in the pan.

A lake with a leaky boat?
About half way.

A fried egg on a hammock.

Why did you get thrown out of the Navy?

I threw a banana skin out of the window.

They threw you out for that?

Well, I was in a submarine at the time.

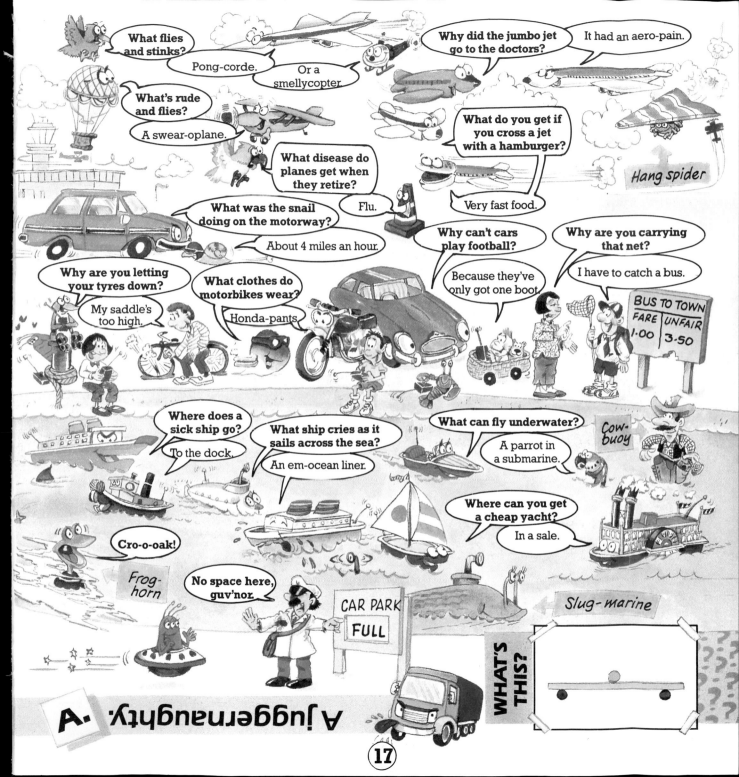

O. What's big, blue and on a diet?

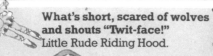

What did the ballerina say in the restaurant?
A table for tu-tu.

What's short, scared of wolves and shouts "Twit-face!"
Little Rude Riding Hood.

What's the world's most musical country?
Tune-isia.

Have you heard about the chocolate factory?
When the sun came out, it melted.

Why did the broom get up in the night?
It couldn't get to sweep.

What do you get if you cross a clock with a thief?
A tick tock-et.

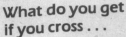

What do you get if you cross . . .

A computer and a banana skin?
A slipped disk.

Some grapes with a baker?
A bunch of flour.

A fridge with an angry monster?
A nasty cold.

If a red house is made of red bricks, what's a green house made of?
Glass.

Which is correct: 9+5 *is* 13, or 9+5 *are* 13?
Neither, it's 14.

That figures.

How do you catch Egyptian flu?
From mummy.

What colour was the retired trumpeter?
Blue.

What's green and goes at 150 mph?
A moss-tang.

Why did the car's wheels explode?
Because they were tyre-d out.

What's the best road on which to eat spaghetti?
One with a fork in it.

Why put your record in the refrigerator?
Because I like to play it cool.

What do you get if you leave your toothpaste in the freezer?
An ice tube.

Call me a taxi! OK – you're a taxi.

DOCTOR DOCTOR

I keep thinking I'm a spider.
Well come down off the ceiling, and let me examine you.

People keep ignoring me.
Next!

I've got invisible sickness.
I'm afraid I can't see you.

I keep getting lost.
You're telling me, this is a Chinese restaurant.

I'm a burglar and I'm sick.
Well you'd better take some medicine.

I've just swallowed a roll of film.
I'm sure nothing serious will develop.

A pea on a skateboard.

THINGS TO EAT WITH **SOUP** by Roland Butter

DINNER'S READY by Carmen Geddit

LOSING WEIGHT by Wilma Clothes-Fitt

ELECTRICIANS WEEKLY — A LOOK AT CURRENT AFFAIRS

Doctor, I've lost my memory. When did this happen?

When did what happen?

How re-volting.

(18)

How old was the girl after her dinner? **Ate.**

How old was the boy who'd beaten his friend at tennis? **One.**

How old was the escaped prisoner with no teeth? **Free.**

There was an old man of Hong Kong,
Who's poems were always too long.
When asked why this was,
He said "It's because
Although I try hard, the last line
always seems to go on & on & on & on...

Why did the umbrella maker work hard? He was saving for a sunny day.

What's worse than raining cats and dogs? Hailing taxis.

Why was there a storm at the funeral? Because of the thunder-takers.

What did the orchestra play more quickly in a storm? Because they had a lightning conductor.

Why didn't the Egyptians build pyramids in the fog? Because they could not see the point.

What weather do archers dread? Mist.

What's green and camps? A boy sprout.

What goes 'hoe hoe'? A happy gardener.

Who's the boss of the hankies? The hanky chief.

What do you call a baker who's mad about bread? A dough-nut.

Where does a general keep his armies? Up his sleevies.

Who was Shakespeare's shortest character? Gnomeo.

Metro-gnome

Why don't gnomes go to the doctors? Because they're always in good elf.

Gnome Sweet Gnome

Any space jokes here? Gnome-mate.

Why are dentists sad? Because they are always looking down in the mouth.

What did the artist do as he died? He drew his last breath.

What do auctioneers say at the hairdressers? Going, going, gone.

What do dentists like best at fun fairs? The molar coaster.

What do you call a gnome's false teeth? Miniatures.

What stands still and goes? A grandfather clock.

Why did the girl throw the kitchen clock? So she could see time fly. Was it second hand?

Why are goalkeepers always at the bank? Because they're good savers.

Heard the joke about my piggy bank? There's nothing in it.

WHAT'S THIS?

A slimming pool. A.

19

What do you do if you find a crocodile in your bed?
Sleep somewhere else.

What was the baby hippo called?
Nappy-potty-mus.

What do you call horses that live next door?
Neigh-bours.

What wobbles and rings?
A jelly-phone.

What did the mouse say to its noisy children?
Squeak when you're squoken to.

What do you get if you cross a stereo with a bluebottle?
Hi-fli.

DOCTOR DOCTOR

I think I'm a waste bin.
Don't talk rubbish.

I can't get to sleep.
Lie on the edge of your bed, you'll soon drop off.

One of these standing on the edge of a lake.

How did you stop your son from biting his nails?
I made him wear shoes.

Do you know what makes ma mad?
The letter "d".

Why did Lucy like the letter "k"?
Because it made her 'Lucky'.

I saw the sun rise today.
So what? Yesterday I saw the kitchen sink.

Do you like the carpet?
No, I wanted a van – and don't call me "pet".

KNOCK! KNOCK! WHO'S THERE?

Dishwasher.
Dishwasher who?
Dishwasher way I shpoke when losht my falshe teeff.

Ammonia.
Ammonia who?
Ammonia a little boy – I can't reach the bell.

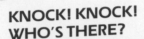

Iona Littlemouse
Pet Street
Hamsterdam
West Gerbilly
N. Americat

Dad! There's an invisible woman at the door.
Tell her I can't see her.

Mum! There's a man with an egg at the door.
Tell him to beat it.

Mum! I've swallowed a light bulb – what shall I do?
Use a candle instead.

FITTING CARPETS by Walter Wall

Baby Sitting BY JUSTIN CASEY HOWLS

The NAUGHTY BOY —by— Enid Spanking

HUSH-A-BYE-BABY by Wendy Bough-breaks

SHARING A BED-ROOM by Constance Noring

AFTER THE HURRICANE —by— Rufus Quick

Q. Where do ghosts play golf?

What do skeleton's put in their cakes?
Skull-tanas.

What do you call a ghost with a hose?
A fire frighter.

What's big, hairy, and goes at twice the speed of sound?
King Kongcorde.

What do you call a ghostly mushroom?
A toads-ghoul.

What do you get if you cross a barber and a ghost?
A scare-dresser.

What did the pretty ghoul enter?
A boo-ty contest.

She didn't stand a ghost of a chance.

Where do ghouls go for their holiday?
The Dead Sea.

There are always a lot of ghost-guards.

Sea-ghoul

Why are ghosts terrible liars?

You can always see through them.

NEWSFLASH

The police have appointed their first ghost. It will be called Chief In-spectre.

Today was the Monster Beauty Contest. As usual there were no winners.

What's a ghost's favourite food?
Spook-hetti.

What's a ghost's favourite story?
Ghouldilocks.

What's a ghost's favourite play?
A phantomime.

What's a ghost's favourite breakfast?
Dreaded wheat.

What position did the ghost play at football? Ghoulkeeper.

I keep seeing into the future.

Really, when did this start?

Next Thursday.

WAITER! WAITER!

What's this gravestone doing in my salad?
It's a tomb-ato.

There's a ghost in my soup.
All right sir, don't make spectre-cle of yourself.

There are some ghosts in my stew.
That's because it's ghoul-ash, sir.

What's a ghost's favourite sweet?
Boo-ble gum.

What are a ghost's favourite trees?
Ceme-trees.

What's a ghost's favourite game?
Hide and shriek.

I thought it was haunt the thimble.

What do ghosts say after a night's haunting?

I'm dead on my feet.

His little brother.

HE RAN IN SCREAMING
by Jess C. Naspook

A HORRID DEATH
by Barry De Lyve

I SAW A SPOOK
by Claire Razz-Day

Ghost train-er

Swimming Ghoul

How does a ghoul start a letter?

Tomb it may concern.

It's delivered by the ghost-man.

22

Where do spies do their shopping?

What's black, wet and hairy?
An oil wig.

Why couldn't the man go to a Stone Age Furs exhibition?
Because it was early clothing.

Who is the patron saint of playgrounds?
St Francis of a see-saw.

What's the world's most shocking city?
Electri-city.

Where do lions buy old clothes?
Jungle sales.

What's stripy, shakes and is found at the North Pole?
A polar zebra.

DOCTOR DOCTOR

I've cut myself, and all you do is tell me jokes.
I want you to be in stitches.

I keep getting smaller.
You'll have to be little patient.

I snore so loudly that I wake myself up.
Well sleep in another room.

I've just eaten a pen.
Here's some pencillen.

My nose is running and my feet smell.
Looks like you're built upside down.

Where do sick alsatians go?
To the dog-tor.

Where do they send sick horses?
To horspital.

Where do kangeroos get their glasses?
At a Hoptitian.

DO **NOT** READ THIS NOTICE

Oi!

KNOCK! KNOCK! WHO'S THERE?

Europe.
Europe who?
Europe early this morning.

Asia.
Asia who?
Bless you!

Jamaica.
Jamaica who?
Jamaica lot of money telling jokes?

There was a young man from Australia,
Who painted his foot like a dahlia.
A penny a look
Was all by the book,
But sixpence a smell was a failure.

NEWSFLASH

A giant and a dwarf have just escaped from prison. Police are looking high and low for them.

At the local shops, some thieves went on the rampage. The police say that the thieves...

Stole some plant food – but they'll root them out.

Stole a mirror – and they're looking into it.

Stole a mattress – and they'll look in the spring.

Stole some soap and a sponge – then made a clean getaway.

Half of one of these.

HEALTH FOODS	TRAVEL AGENTS	PHOTOGRAPHERS	MUSIC SHOP	SHIPBUILDERS	CLOCK REPAIRS
CLOSED DUE TO SICKNESS	GONE ON HOLIDAY	Back in a flash	BACK IN A MINUET	Gone to Launch	BACK IN A TICK

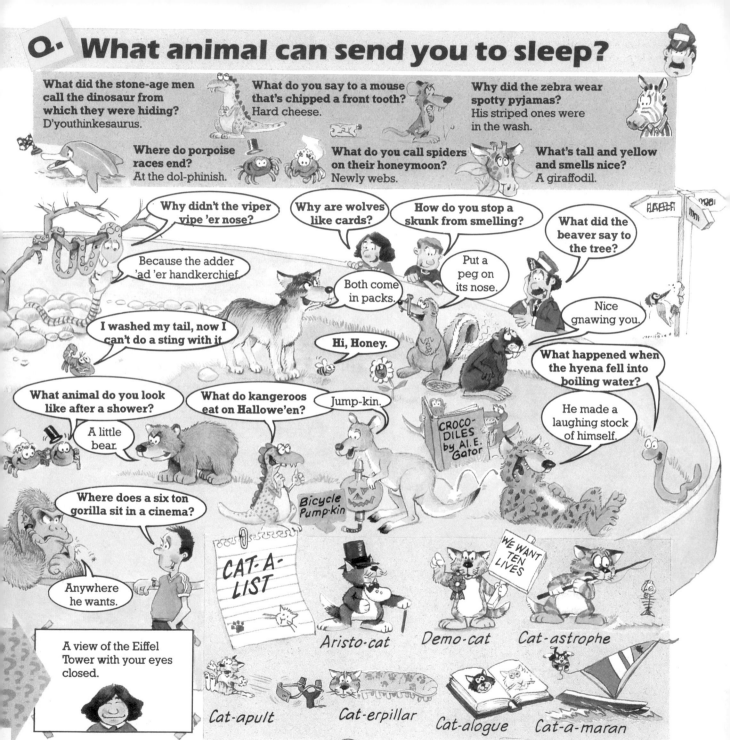

What did the stone-age men call the dinosaur from which they were hiding? D'youthinkesaurus.

What do you say to a mouse that's chipped a front tooth? Hard cheese.

Why did the zebra wear spotty pyjamas? His striped ones were in the wash.

Where do porpoise races end? At the dol-phinish.

What do you call spiders on their honeymoon? Newly webs.

What's tall and yellow and smells nice? A giraffodil.

Why didn't the viper vipe 'er nose?

Why are wolves like cards?

How do you stop a skunk from smelling?

What did the beaver say to the tree?

Because the adder 'ad 'er handkerchief.

Both come in packs.

Put a peg on its nose.

Nice gnawing you.

I washed my tail, now I can't do a sting with it

Hi, Honey.

What happened when the hyena fell into boiling water?

What animal do you look like after a shower?

What do kangeroos eat on Hallowe'en?

Jump-kin.

He made a laughing stock of himself.

A little bear.

CROCO-DILES by Al. E. Gator

Where does a six ton gorilla sit in a cinema?

Bicycle Pump-kin

Anywhere he wants.

A view of the Eiffel Tower with your eyes closed.

CAT-A-LIST

WE WANT TEN LIVES

Aristo-cat

Demo-cat

Cat-astrophe

Cat-apult

Cat-erpillar

Cat-alogue

Cat-a-maran

26

Can an elephant jump higher than a lamppost?

Yes, lampposts can't jump.

What does a buffalo say when her son leaves?

Bi-son.

Why do giraffes have long legs and necks?

In case they have smelly feet.

What's the difference between a wet day and a tiger with a toothache?

I can't understand what he's saying.

That's because he's a mumble bee.

One pours with rain, the other roars with pain.

What do you need to know to be a lion tamer?

A bit more than the lion.

Why can't you play cards in the jungle?

There are too many cheetahs.

WAITER! WAITER! Do you serve crabs?

We serve anyone, sir.

What's that fly doing in my ice cream?

Shivering.

What do dogs write on walls? Woofiti.

How do chickens dance? Chick to chick.

What do you get if you cross a snowball with a shark? Frostbite.

What's green and smells? A frog's nose.

Why did the boa constrictors marry? They had a crush on each other.

Heard about the famous cow? She was in the moo-vies.

What happened when the cat swallowed a ball of wool? She had mittens.

What's the definition of . . .

An octupus? An eight sided cat.

Politics? A parrot that's swallowed a watch.

A snail? A slug in a crash helmet.

Here's your lipstick, madam.

Put it on my bill.

Where do Chinese wasps come from? Stingapore.

I want to look at the Milky Whale.

Jelly-scope

Flying snore-cer

ZZZZ

KEEP GOING

A. A hypno-potomus.

WHAT'S THIS?

Who is Santa Claus' wife?

Custard SPY

TOYS

What do you call a gun with three barrels?
A trifle.

What athlete is made of wool?
A long jumper.

Why do boomerangs never go out of fashion?
Because they're always making a comeback.

Who wears a crown and climbs ladders?
A window queen-er.

How can you cut the sea?
With a see-saw.

What's the laziest thing in a doctor's bag?
The sleeping pills.

KNOCK! KNOCK! WHO'S THERE?

Henrietta.
Henrietta who?
Henry ate a boiled egg.

Tish.
Tish who?
Got a cold?

Francis.
Francis who?
Francis full of French people.

Safari.
Safari who?
Safari so goodie.

Why didn't the clown work in the winter?
Because he only did summersaults.

When is a clown's face like a story?
When it's made up.

How does a clown dress on a cold day?
Quickly.

What's the quickest way to the station?
Run fast.

Last night I dreamt I was talking to world's cleverest person.
Oh yes, what did I say?

This painting is over 100 years old.
Did you do it?

This morning I had to get up and answer the telephone in my pyjamas.
Funny place to have a telephone.

Your parents have got three children, haven't they?
No, only me – and two spares.

Napoleon Boneypart

THE POLICEMAN'S TEST by Courtney Crooks

What instrument is like a gun?
A bang-jo.

What's an opera star's favourite place?
Singer-pore.

Which composer ran round castles?
Moat-zart.

It was too flat.

Why wasn't the tyre allowed in the choir?

A snake doing a somersault.

What's the difference between a postbox, a canary and a fishing rod?
I don't know.

You can post a letter in a postbox but not a canary.
But what about the fishing rod?

Thought that would catch you.

Where do firemen go when they get hurt?
To a hose-pital.

Why do firemen wear red belts?
To hold their trousers up.

Why do firemen enjoy climbing ladders?
Because they like to go up in the world.

Someone say "adders"?

Ambul-ants

I wish I could spit like that.

These vegetables are funny.
That's because they're arti-jokes.

Where did this hearing aid in my salad come from?
Pardon?

Why is there a moth in my soup?
Because we've run out of flies.

This coffee is strong.
Well you said you wanted something to pick you up.

Do you want to leave a tip?
Yes – serve the food more quickly.

There once was a gardener from Leeds
Who swallowed a packet of seeds.
A big yellow rose
Grew out of his nose,
And his beard was a tangle of weeds.

What do you find in the middle of India?
The letter "d".

What's always in fashion, but always out of date?
The letter "f".

What do you say when you get off a boat?
Thank you ferry much.

What does golf begin with?
A tee.

What do calculators always say?
You can count on me.

What begins with "p" and has hundred's of letters?
Postman.

Why do basketball players have long arms?
Because if they were any shorter they wouldn't reach their hands.

How many ears did Davy Crocket have?
Three: left, right and a wild frontier.

MNX   ABNAP   PNO

What do you call . . .

A girl who asks questions? Wanda.

A girl who looks like a parrot? Polly.

A boy with a seagull on his head? Cliff.

A girl who behaves like a mouse? Nora.

A boy with a paper bag on head? Russell

A girl who's a real creep? Ivy.

A boy who is a thief? Robin.

A girl who blows hard? Gail.

Did you hear about the karate expert who joined the army?
The first time he saluted, he killed himself.

Why is a pillow like a general's office?
They're both headquarters.

What's above a general?
His hat.

Who has the biggest boots in the Indian army?
The soldier with the biggest feet.

Is this the page about space?

I'm a sergeant, not a star-gent.

Did you hear about the plastic surgeon?
He sat in front of the fire and melted.

Gran says I have my mum's nose and my dad's eyes.
Who's got yours then?

A.

Mary Christmas.

Santa claws

On these two pages are some ideas for ways to make up your own jokes.

Jokes using a word which has two meanings

There are some words which mean two completely different things. Below is a flow chart which will help you use them to make up a joke.

| Find a word with two meanings. | → | A date. |

| Write down the two things that the word means in similar phrases. | → | A palm tree has dates. (Fruit) A calender has dates. (Days) |

| Ask why the two things are like each other to make your joke. | → | **Why is a palm tree like a calender?** Because they both have lots of dates. |

Jokes using words which sound the same, but are spelled differently.

There are also words which sound exactly the same, but which are spelled differently.

| Write down the two words. | → | Word 1: red Word 2: read |

| Describe something using word 1, such as: A . . . . has a (word 1). A . . . . is (word 1). | → | A fire engine is red. |

| Describe something using the same type of question, and word 2. | → | A book is read. |

| Ask a question which includes the two things. | → | **Why is a fire engine like a book?** Because they are both read (red). |

This kind of joke works well when you say it, because the other person won't be able to see the two words are spelled differently.

Here are two lists of words which you can use to make up jokes like the ones above.

Words which have two meanings

Pen
Spring
Stable
Nail
Pack
Sink
Right
Scales

Beam
Top
Post
Duck
Plug
Pipe
Ring
Stamp

Bank
Swallow
Palm
Club
Bar
Saw
Pipe
Tip

Bill
Glasses
Ball
Fire
Match
Rock
Tape
Recorder

Words which sound the same but are spelled differently.

Queue – Cue
Right – Write
Weigh – Way
Sail – Sale
Sun – Son
Pair – Pear
Whole – Hole

Bear – Bare
Fir – Fur
Rain – Reign
Tale – Tail
Tax – Tacks
Sore – Saw
Great – Grate

Fair – Fare
Hair – Hare
Tire – Tyre
Stair – Stare
Plain – Plane
Tow – Toe
Shake – Sheik

Jokes using words which sound similar

Some jokes are funny because all or part of a word is replaced by another word which sounds like it. This is called a pun. For example: Where do rowing boats go when they are ill? To an oars-pital. Below is a flow chart which shows you how to make up pun jokes.

Write down a word which may have other words which sound similar to it. This is the Jokeword. → Quack

Write one or two new words which rhyme with it, or sound very similar. → Track Crack

Can you think of a way in which one of the new words is normally used? → Railway Tracks

No
Try again with two new words. **Yes**

Write the Jokeword in place of word 2. This will be the idea for the answer to the joke. → Railway quacks

Think up a question which uses the areas from which the two words come. → i.e. Ducks and trains

What do duck trains run on? Railway quacks.

Jokes using an 'odd' idea

You can make a joke by imagining an everyday object in an odd situation. The flow chart below tells you how.

Write down a well known object. → A plane

What it's like

Write two things which describe it: → Has wheels

What it does

Flies

Write down an odd activity that your object could never do. → Go on a trampoline.

Describe one thing about this activity. → Bouncing up and down.

Write a joke using the three descriptions. The answer will be your original object doing the odd activity. → What has wheels, flies and bounces up and down?

A plane on a trampoline.

But you haven't said anything about space jokes.

Next page.

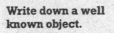

Q. What do you call a space wizard?

What did the astronomer use to get out of prison?
A tel-escape.

Why was the mouse nibbling the planet?
Because it was in gnaw-bit.

What's a planet's favourite drink?
Gravi-tea.

What floats in space and looks like a donkey?
An ass-teroid.

Why are false teeth like stars?
Because they come out at night.

Where do space bees go when they get married?
On honey-moon.

What do astronauts carry their sandwiches in?
A launch box.

What do you call a koala from outer space?
An austr-alien.

Where do astronauts park their spaceships?
On a parking meteor.

Why do astronauts like American football?
Because they're good at touch-downs.

What's an alien's favourite sweet?
Martian-mallows.

What fish do you find in space?
Star-fish.

How do you get a baby astronaut to sleep?
Rocket.

What's a crab's favourite planet?
Niptune.

What do space teachers always carry?
Their regi-star.

What's sweet, yellow and orbits the sun?
Mars-ipan.

What sea is in space?
The galax-sea.

What do astronauts use to play badminton with?
Space shuttle-cock.

What did the hungry astronomer say?
I'm star-ving.

Which planet is never hungry?
A full moon.

What is the most polluted planet?
Pollut-o.

What do you call a flying saucer in hot fat?
An unidentified frying object.

Why is the planet Saturn like a telephonist?
They're both surrounded by rings.

What do astronaut archers aim at?
The star-get.

What did one shooting star say to another?
Pleased to meteor.

A BUMPY TOUCH-DOWN by Paul Anding

SPACE INVADERS by A. Leanne Zahir

SPACE WEAPONS BY Ray Gunne

Eggs-tra terrestrial

What's the matter with you?

I've got smelly feet.

WELCOME DAMIEN THE ALIEN!

Heard any good jokes lately?

Why is the sky high?
So birds don't bump their heads.

What bird is found in space?
A star-ling.

What do cows say at night?
Mooooon.

A. A flying saucerer.

(32)